I'M IN THE SPOTLIGHT!

I'M IN THE SPOTLIGHT!

A JOURNAL OF DISCOVERY
FOR YOUNG WRITERS

by
Mary Euretig

DREAM
TREE
PRESS

Sacramento, California

I'M IN THE SPOTLIGHT!

A JOURNAL OF DISCOVERY FOR YOUNG WRITERS

by Mary Euretig

Published by:

DREAM
TREE
PRESS

Copyright ©1993 by Mary Euretig
First Printing 1993
Printed in the United States of America

ISBN 0-9628216-1-6

Additional copies of *I'M IN THE SPOTLIGHT!* are available by contacting:
DREAM TREE PRESS
3836 Thornwood Drive
Sacramento, CA 95821
1-800-769-9029

To my parents,
who taught me the first and most
important lessons of life

and

To Joseph, Andrew, Matthew, and Kristen,
who are always in the spotlight

TABLE OF CONTENTS

Dear Parents,

Children have important things to say and enjoy expressing their thoughts in writing if given the opportunity to do so in a risk-free environment. This book provides a forum for young writers to respond to various aspects of their world. Your child will experience the satisfaction which comes from being able to write fluently on topics of interest as they complete the journal.

Your help may be needed with certain portions of the book, particularly the chapter on "Early Memories." This will give you a chance to retrieve the baby pictures and share some of those past times with your young writer.

When *I'M IN THE SPOTLIGHT* is completed, you will have samples of handwriting, artwork, and written expression in one convenient place. Those who treasure their child's written and artistic expression will consider this completed book a priceless memento.

Show enthusiasm and listen attentively when you child reads a selection. Who knows? There may be a budding author in your family!

Mary Euretig

Dear Boys and Girls,

This book is about a very important person . . . you!

It contains chapters where you will have a chance to write about yourself, your family, and friends. In other chapters you will record your feelings, school experiences, favorite things, and future plans. You can draw pictures to go with your writing on many of the pages. At the end of every chapter there are blank pages for you to write about whatever you choose.

In this journal, do not worry about using your best handwriting and spelling words correctly. It is more important to record your thoughts and feelings and to have fun while doing it.

Be sure to save *I'M IN THE SPOTLIGHT.* It will be an important keepsake which you will enjoy having when you are an adult.

Have fun and happy writing!

Your friend,

Benedict

ACKNOWLEDGEMENTS

Special thanks to:

Diane Conway and her students
at Deterding School in Carmichael, California,
for allowing me to use their classroom
as a laboratory for this book.

Dale and Bob Reinhard for once again sharing
their expertise with me.

Lisa Bacchini for her cover and text design
and illustration.

Matthew Euretig for naming the book.

Kristen Euretig for giving me her expert opinion
on many of the topics and prompts.

Andrew Euretig for being a terrific teenager during
the writing of this book.

Joe Euretig for his second opinion on every page.

THE SPOTLIGHT'S ON . . .

ME, MYSELF, & I

Vital Statistics

My name is _____ _____ _____.
                        first   middle   last

My parents chose this name for me because _____

_____.

Just for the record, I am _____ years old.

My hair is _____ and my eyes are _____.

I am _____ inches tall and weigh _____ pounds.

People say I look like

_____

_____.

I like these things about
the way I look:

_____

_____

_____.

If I could change one thing
about the way I look it
would be _____

_____.

SELF-PORTRAIT

Personality

I am different than anyone else.
These are things I like about myself.

_____   _____

_____   _____

_____   _____

I asked my parents what they liked best about me and
they said, "_____

_____."

I asked three of my friends what they liked best about me
and this is what I found out:

_____ likes _____
      name

_____ likes _____
      name

_____ likes _____
      name

There is one thing about myself I would like to change and
that is _____.

I think this change could happen if _____

_____.

My Home

I live in _____, _____.
 city   state

My address is _____ _____.
                      number   street name

This is how I would describe my home.

_____

_____

```
┌─────────────────────────────────────────────────┐
│                                  ┌──────────────┐ │
│                                  │ My home has  │ │
│                                  │ _____ bedrooms, │
│                                  │ _____ windows, │ │
│                                  │ and _____ doors.│
│                                  └──────────────┘ │
│                                                   │
│                    ┌──────────────┐               │
│                    │   MY HOME    │               │
└────────────────────└──────────────┘───────────────┘
```

The very best thing about my home is _____

_____

The most unusual thing about my home is _____

_____

If I could change something about my home it would be

_____

My Room

The room in which I sleep is painted _____.

The cover on my bed is _____.

I keep _____, _____,

and _____ on shelves in my room.

These are pictures of things on the walls of my room:

I like my room because _____.

Something unusual about my room is _____

_____.

If I could change one thing about my room it would be

_____

_____.

 My Neighborhood

This is a list of things I like about our neighborhood.

_____   _____

_____   _____

_____   _____

My favorite neighbor is _____
because _____.

Our most unusual neighbor is _____
because_____.

The best looking house in our neighborhood belongs to the
_____ family.

Our neighborhood would be a better place to live if _____
_____.

| A MAP OF MY STREET |

My Family's Car

FAMILY CAR

LICENSE PLATE

The car I ride in most often is a _____ _____.
                                      year   name of car

I like it because_____.

_____ is the person who drives it most often.

When I grow up I want to drive a _____
                                            name of car

because _____.

_____

_____

_____

_____

_____

_____

_____

_____

_____

_____

THE SPOTLIGHT'S ON . . .

EARLY MEMORIES

The Beginning

I was born on _____ _____, _____,
                    month   day   year

at _____ Hospital.

**Place newborn
photo here**

I weighed _____ pounds and was _____ inches long.

When my parents first saw me they thought I looked like

_____.

These people came to see me when I was born:

_____   _____

_____   _____

I asked my parents to tell me what I was like those first few
days in the hospital. This is what they said:

_____

_____

_____.

My first home was at _____
                              street address
in _____, _____.
         city   state

Babyhood

A lot of things changed around the house when my parents brought me home from the hospital. These are three of them:

1. _____
   _____

2. _____
   _____

3. _____
   _____

**Place baby
photo here**

I liked to eat _____ when I was a baby and my favorite toy was a _____.

My first visit to a doctor was when I was _____ months old because _____.

One of the cutest things I did when I was a baby was _____ _____.

I really gave my parents a scare one time when I _____ _____.

Sometimes the only thing that would calm me down when I was a baby was _____.

Toddler Time

I learned how to walk when I was _____ months old.

Place toddler photo here

My first word was

_____

and I said it when I was about _____ months old.

Once I began to walk, nothing in the house was safe. I used to drive my parents crazy because I was always getting into _____.

The book I liked to have my parents read to me when I was little was _____.

I entertained myself by _____ _____.

My parents wanted to give me away one time when I _____ _____.

I asked my parents to tell me three words that described me as a toddler and they said _____, _____, and _____.

Growing Up

I went off to preschool when I was _____ years old. The school

was _____ and my teacher

was _____.

Activities I did at school were:

_____
activity

_____
activity

Some of the friends I played with were _____,

_____, and _____.

I really liked to have _____

read to me when I was this age.

A game my parents used to play with me was _____

_____.

I was awfully cute when I was little. Something funny that my

parents told me I did was _____.

The Spotlight's On . . .

... My Own Thoughts

_____

_____

_____

_____

_____

_____

_____

_____

_____

_____

THE SPOTLIGHT'S ON . . .

FAMILY MATTERS

My Family Tree

first

middle

last

Me

first

middle

last

Dad

first

middle

last

Mom

first

middle

last

Dad's Father

first

middle

last

Dad's Mother

first

middle

last

Mom's Father

first

middle

last

Mom's Mother

18

My Family

I live in a family and these are the people who live with me:

_____   _____

_____   _____

_____   _____

Three words which describe my family are _____,

_____, and _____.

These are the activities my family likes to do together:

_____   _____

_____   _____

The best part about being in my family is _____

_____.

If I could change one thing about my family, it would be

_____.

FAMILY PORTRAIT

Family Rules

My family has the following rules:

1. _____

2. _____

3. _____

The one I have the most trouble following is _____

_____.

If I break an important rule, I might get a punishment of

_____.

One rule I think our family should have is _____

_____.

If I want to please my father,
I would _____

_____.

If I want to please my mother,
I would _____

_____.

A bad habit I have which annoys my family is

_____

_____.

Something happens in our family which I think is unfair. It is

_____

_____.

I think I'm lucky to have my family because _____

_____.

Mother

My mother's full name is:

_____ _____ _____
first   middle   last

She was born in:

_____, _____, _____
city   state   country

Her birthday is: _____, _____, _____
month   day   year

When my mother was my age she liked to play

_____.

She attended _____ school and her favorite
kind of books were _____.
Her best friend was _____.
Her favorite television show was _____.
My mother's main job is _____.
In her free time she likes to _____.
These are some things my mother does for our family:

_____ _____

_____ _____

I think the very best thing about my mother is _____

_____.

The most important lesson I have learned from my mother is

_____

_____.

Father

My father's full name is:

_____   _____   _____
first   middle   last

He was born in:

_____, _____, _____
city   state   country

His birthday is: _____, _____, _____
                                          month   day   year

When my father was my age he liked to play

_____.

He attended _____ school and his favorite
kind of books were _____.
His best friend was _____.
His favorite television show was _____.
My father's main job is _____.
In his free time he likes to _____.
These are some things my father does for our family:

_____   _____

_____   _____

I think the very best thing about my father is _____

_____.

The most important lesson I have learned from my father is

_____

_____.

Memories

Our family has taken trips together.

The one I enjoyed the most was _____

because _____.

We have had some happy times together.

I remember once when we _____

_____.

Something sad happened in our family.

This is what happened: _____

_____.

Weekend Fun

On Saturdays my family usually _____

_____.

On Sundays my family usually _____

_____.

Our family celebrates these holidays:

HOLIDAY   HOW WE CELEBRATE

_____   _____

_____   _____

_____   _____

 Extended Family

My mother has _____ sister(s) and _____ brother(s).

My father has _____ sister(s) and _____ brother(s).

My mother's and father's brothers and sisters
are my aunts and uncles.

I have a total of _____ aunts and _____ uncles.

Their children are my cousins. I have _____ cousins.

My favorite cousin is _____ because

_____.

The cousin closest to my age is _____.

The one I see most often is _____.

The one who lives farthest away from me is _____.

Here is something interesting
about some of my aunts and uncles.

Aunt _____

_____

Aunt _____

_____

Uncle _____

_____

Uncle _____

_____

Interview

It is interesting to interview a grandparent or an older person because life was very different when they were my age.

Name of person interviewed:

_____ _____ _____
first   middle   last

Interview Questions And Answers:

When were you born? _____

Where did you grow up? _____

What schools did you attend? _____

_____

Who were your best friends? _____

_____

What did you like about school? _____

_____

What did you dislike about school? _____

_____

What games did you like to play? _____

_____

What did you enjoy reading? _____

_____

What were your favorite foods? _____

_____

Interview

Can you tell about a time when you were punished and why?

_____

_____

What kinds of things were happening in the news when you were my age?

_____

_____

How old were you when you left home? _____

Where did you go? _____

_____

_____

When did you get married? _____

How did you meet your spouse? _____

_____

_____

What was the most important lesson you learned when you were young? _____

_____

If you could change one thing about your life, what would it be?

_____

Is there some advice you would like to give me?

_____

_____

THE SPOTLIGHT'S ON . . .

FRIENDS, BUDDIES, PALS

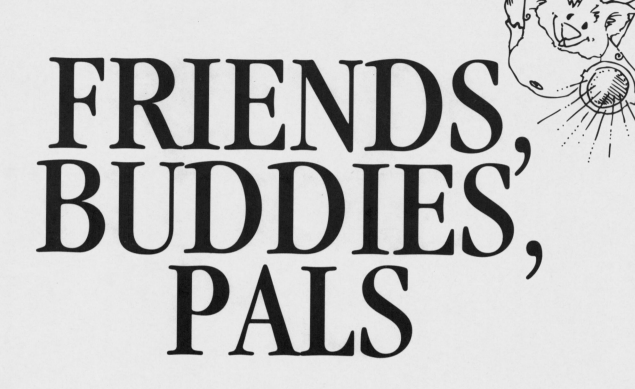

Forever Friends

In my opinion, a friend is someone who _____

_____.

The very first friend I ever had was _____ when
I was ____ years old. When we got together we usually
played _____.

I have had many friends over the years.
Here is a list of the ones I remember:

_____   _____

_____   _____

_____   _____

You can show friendship by _____

_____.

If someone wants to be my friend they should never

_____.

I got into trouble with _____ for
                                      friend

_____.

A friend once hurt my feelings by _____

_____.

I know I hurt one of my friend's feelings when I _____

_____.

Best Of Friends

Sometimes I would rather play with one certain friend and at other times, I would choose a different friend. I enjoy being with friends for different reasons.

This is a list of the three friends I play with most often and the activities we enjoy together:

FRIEND   ACTIVITY

_____   _____

_____   _____

_____   _____

Right now the person who is probably my best friend is

_____ .

This is how I met that person:

_____

_____

_____ .

MY BEST FRIEND

Three words I would choose to describe my friend are

_____, _____,

and _____ .

Good Times

These are activities I enjoy when I am playing with a group of friends:

_____   _____

_____   _____

_____   _____

The friend whose house I go to most often is _____
because _____.
If I get to choose, I would most like to go to _____
house because _____.

Sometimes I spend the night at a friend's house. The most fun I
ever had was when I stayed at _____ house. This
is what we did: _____
_____.

If I had a party, these are the friends I would like to invite:

_____   _____

_____   _____

_____   _____

The party I attended at _____ house was the most fun.
This is what we did: _____
_____
_____.

Awards

If I were handing out friendship awards, these friends would be the winners:

Best sense of humor .... _____

Most patient .... _____

Person I'd trust with a secret ..... _____

Most talkative .... _____

Best dressed .... _____

Most adventurous .... _____

Most popular .... _____

Smartest .... _____

Best looking .... _____

Most athletic .... _____

Best artist .... _____

Most polite .... _____

Neatest .... _____

There are other awards that I would like to give:

AWARD   NAME OF FRIEND

_____ to _____

_____ to _____

_____ to _____

33

The Spotlight's On . . .

THE SPOTLIGHT'S ON . . .

MY FAVORITE THINGS

Books

The type of books I enjoy reading most are _____
_____ .

One of my very favorite books is _____
_____ by _____ .

My favorite part is when _____
_____ .

If I could be any character from a book I would like to be:

CHARACTER	BOOK

I would like to see authors write more books about

_____ .

Someday I might like to write a book about

_____ .

If someone wants to give me a book for a gift, I would ask for

_____ .

Music

The music I like best is _____.

My favorite song is _____

by _____.

These are the words to the first part of my favorite song:

_____

_____

_____

My favorite singer is _____.

The group I like best is _____.

I asked three friends to tell me their favorite song:

FRIEND   FAVORITE SONG

_____   _____

_____   _____

_____   _____

If I could play a musical instrument, I would like to play the _____.

I think it would be fun because _____

_____

_____.

INSTRUMENT

38

Television

My favorite television show is _____.

These are the actors and actresses on the show:

_____   _____

_____   _____

_____ is the actor/actress I like best

because _____.

This show comes on at _____ on _____.
                                     time   day

Other shows on television which I watch and enjoy are

_____, _____,

and _____.

The best commercial on T.V. is one for _____.

I usually watch my TV programs in the _____ room.

> We have _____ television sets in our house. I watch about _____ hours of television a week.

MY FAVORITE TV PROGRAM

Sports

This is a list of sports that I enjoy playing:

_____   _____

_____   _____

My favorite one is _____ because

_____.

One sport I think would be fun to try is _____.

A sports figure I admire is _____

because _____.

He/she plays for the _____.
                                                    team
If I played a professional sport I would choose _____

because _____.

MY FAVORITE UNIFORM

Food

I like to eat! This is a list of my favorite foods:

_____   _____

_____   _____

_____   _____

The junk food I like best is _____.

My favorite healthy food is _____.

If my parents asked me to choose a restaurant for dinner, I would

pick _____

and I would order _____.

I know how to prepare a few foods.

_____ is my specialty.

This is my idea of a perfect meal:

MENU

Toys And Games

This is a picture of my favorite stuffed animal which is a _____ _____.

Its name is _____ _____.

Three words which describe my animal are _____, _____, and _____.

STUFFED ANIMAL

This is a list of my favorite toys:

_____ _____

_____ _____

If I am playing with a friend, we usually choose to play with

_____.
toy

If I am playing alone, I would probably play with

_____.
toy

The board game I enjoy the most is _____.

I usually play it with _____ and _____.

My favorite card game is _____.

Odds And Ends

My favorite color is _____ and my lucky number is _____.

One of the best movies I have seen recently is _____ _____ with _____ and _____.

I liked it because _____ _____.

My favorite kind of clothes are _____, _____, and _____.

The shoes I like to wear most are_____.

The hair style I look best in is _____.

FAVORITE OUTFIT

My favorite kind of weather is _____ because _____.

The season of the year I enjoy most is _____.

_____ is the animal I like best. It is my favorite because _____.

The Spotlight's On . . .

THE SPOTLIGHT'S ON . . .

A RAINBOW OF FEELINGS

Disappointment

I feel disappointed when something I'm planning to do doesn't work out for one reason or another.

I remember a time when I was very disappointed. This is what happened:

_____

_____

_____.

It helps to have a way to handle disappointment. Here is a way I could cheer myself up.

I think my parents were disappointed in me when I _____

_____.

When I disappoint my parents I feel _____

_____.

Something that happened in school which disappointed me:

_____.

Happiness

**Happiness is that wonderful feeling you get
when everything in your life is going along very well.**

When I am happy I feel like _____.

I like to share my happy feelings with _____.

_____ is a place where I usually feel happy.

On the happiest day I can remember, this is what happened:

_____

_____

Here are some pictures of things which make me happy:

_____   _____   _____

A book I read with a happy ending was _____

_____.

This is how it ended: _____

_____.

Anger

Anger is a feeling I get when I am very mad at someone or something.

When I am angry I feel like _____

_____.

When I have a disagreement with someone and can't work it out, I feel angry. These are the people with whom I have the most disagreements:

PERSON   THINGS WE DISAGREE ABOUT

_____   _____

_____   _____

_____   _____

One good way I have learned to settle a disagreement is to

_____.

If I am very angry with someone I could write that person a note to tell them how I feel and why.

Dear _____,

_____

_____

_____

                          From, _____

Fear

Everyone is afraid of certain things.

This is a list of things which scare me:

_____   _____

_____   _____

Here is a picture of something that might frighten me.

[ ]

When I was little I used to be afraid of_____

_____but I'm not anymore.

A time I felt very scared was _____

_____.

A book I read which had a scary part was _____

_____.

I will describe the scary part: _____

_____

_____.

Sadness

**Sadness is a feeling people get when they feel left out,
when they lose someone or something,
or when someone they like is mad at them.**

Sometimes I feel sad because _____
_____.

Something in the news that made me feel sad was _____
_____.

_____ is the name of a movie I saw
which had a sad part. This is what happened in the movie:
_____
_____.

Sometimes when I am sad, crying makes me feel better.

I cried one time when _____.

One way I have learned to cheer myself up is to _____
_____.

If I am sad and someone wants to comfort me, this is what helps
the most: _____.

This is something sad which happened to our family:
_____.

If someone I know is sad, I could try and help by _____

_____.

More Feelings

I feel proud when I know I have done my best.

I felt proud in school when _____

_____.

I know my parents were proud of me when _____

_____.

Embarrassment is what I feel when I have done something that makes me want to run and hide.

I remember feeling embarrassed when _____

_____.

Everyone has embarrassing moments.

I asked one of my parents to tell me one of theirs.

_____

_____

_____.

I feel surprised when something happens which I did not expect.

I was surprised on my birthday one year because

_____.

One of the biggest surprises I've ever had was when

_____.

I surprised someone one time when I _____

_____.

THE SPOTLIGHT'S ON . . .

SCHOOL DAYS, SCHOOL DAYS

My School

The name of my school is _____.

The school was named for _____.

The best thing about my school is _____
_____
_____.

MY SCHOOL

Here are some ways my school could be improved:

_____

_____

_____

_____

My Classroom

I am in the _____ grade. My room number is _____.

My favorite subjects in school are:

_____   _____

_____   _____

_____   _____

My classroom has _____windows, _____ doors, and _____ bulletin boards.

There are _____ students in my classroom.

These are pictures of things on the walls of my classroom.

My Teacher

My teacher's name is _____.

I like my teacher because_____.

Some things I would like my teacher to know about me:

_____

_____

_____

_____

Some things I would like to know about my teacher are:

_____

_____

_____

_____

The best compliment my teacher gave me was _____

_____

_____.

I was punished once for _____

_____.

This is my teacher's favorite expression, "_____

_____."

I wish my teacher would not_____

_____.

If I were the teacher I would spend more time _____

_____

_____.

School Lunch

The place in our school where children eat lunch is called

_____. I eat lunch at

_____. If I buy lunch at school it costs _____.
time of day

People I usually sit with at lunchtime are _____,

_____, and _____.

At lunch we talk about_____

_____.

This is my idea of a perfect lunch:

One thing I dislike eating for lunch is_____.

After lunch my friends and I usually_____

_____.

Playground

You will find these things on the playground at our school.

_____   _____

_____   _____

_____   _____

My favorite thing to do on the playground is_____.

I usually play with _____ and _____.

```
┌─────────────────────────────────────────────────┐
│                                                   │
│                                                   │
│                                                   │
│                                                   │
│                                                   │
│                                                   │
│                  ┌──────────────┐                 │
│                  │  PLAYGROUND  │                 │
└──────────────────┴──────────────┴─────────────────┘
```

Playground Rules

1. _____

2. _____

3. _____

If a rule is broken,_____

_____.

School Workers

It takes many people to make our school run well.

Our school principal is named _____

and the principal's job is to_____

_____.

_____ is the school secretary. The secretary's

job is to_____

_____.

We have a custodian named _____

and the custodian's job is to_____

_____.

Other important people who work in our school are:

NAME   JOB

_____   _____

_____   _____

_____   _____

_____   _____

The job at school I would most like to have is_____

because_____.

The job at school I would like least is_____

because_____.

... My Own Thoughts

THE SPOTLIGHT'S ON . . .

WISHES, HOPES, & DREAMS

Teenage Years

I will be sixteen years old just _____ years from now.

I think I will be going to _____ School.

Activities I would like to do in high school are _____,

_____, and _____.

When I am sixteen I think my parents will finally let me

_____.

They will probably expect me to take more responsibility
around the house. I may have to _____

_____.

One good thing about being a
teen-ager will be _____

_____

_____.

Something which might not
be so good is _____

_____

_____.

MY TEENAGE LOOK

All Grown Up

It's fun to imagine what my life will be like when I am an adult. I will be thirty years old _____ years from now. I think I will be living in _____, _____.
                              city   state

MY FUTURE HOUSE

This is how I think I will spend my free time when I am older:

_____

_____

My social activities will definitely include _____

_____.

Some things I could do to help others who aren't as lucky as I am would be: _____

_____

My Own Children

When I grow up I would like to have ____ children of my own. These are names I would choose for my children:

BOYS   GIRLS

_____   _____

_____   _____

_____   _____

I will take them places like _____,
_____, and _____.

Some stories I will read to them when they are young are:

1. _____

2. _____

3. _____

I will teach them to _____.

I will never _____.

If they misbehave, I will punish them by _____
_____.

Some games I will play with my children are _____
_____.

When my children are the same age as I am now, their allowance will be _____.

My Future Job

When I grow up, I would like to be a _____.

In order to train for this job, I will have to _____
_____.

I think that will take about _____ years.

DRESSED FOR MY JOB

The place where I would most like to work is _____
_____.

The most important thing to think about when you take a job
is _____.

I expect to make about $_____ each month when I am an adult.

This will give me enough money to do the things I like to do
such as _____, _____,
and _____.

Faraway Places

If I could visit three different countries, I would choose:

1. _____

2. _____

3. _____

My idea of a dream vacation would be to go to _____

_____.

I would like to take these people with me: _____

_____

I should be sure and pack the following items:

_____   _____

_____   _____

I think I will need about $_____ to take with me.

Some things that I would like to see and do while I'm on the

trip are _____, _____,

and _____.

My Country

I love my country! The best thing about living here is

_____.

┌─────────────────────────────────────┐
│   │
│   │
│   │
│   │
│   ┌──────────────────┐   │
│   │   MY FLAG   │   │
└──────────┴──────────────────┴───────┘

In my opinion, the most important problem facing our country
is _____.

I think our government could help the problem by _____
_____.

One thing I heard about in the news which bothers me is
_____.

Something which is happening in another country which
makes me feel badly is _____
_____.

Our country would be a better place to live if _____
_____.

I do my part now to help make our country a better place to
live by _____.

Personal Letter

I would like to write a letter to the leader of our country and explain how I feel about the way the country is being run, both good and bad. I will offer some ideas for change. This is what I would write:

Dear _____,

_____

_____

_____

_____

_____

                    From,

                    _____